W9-AFO-839

This Book Belongs To:

_____

Date:

_____

From

The Tragedy of Romeo and Juliet

by

William Shakespeare

Shakespeare for Children:
The Story of Romeo and Juliet

by
Cass Foster

Illustrated by Lisa Molyneux

Consultant/Dramaturg
Suzan L. Zeder

Dedicated to

Dad

Danny and Mark

Acknowledgements

The author would like to thank the following individuals for their contributions (directly or indirectly) to the development of this book:

Yolanda Allen, Gail Bird, Sandy Boggs, Professor John Coldewey, Ph.D., University of Washington; Mary Court, Lynn Dominick, The Editor's Desk; Terri Fisher, Ph.D., The Ohio State University at Mansfield; Mary Gilmore of GraphicWorks, Marcella Grau, Laura Grimm, Professor Lynn Johnson, Ph.D., Program Administrator of Early Childhood Development, The Ohio State University at Mansfield; Professor Rick Kohler, Ph.D., The Ohio State University at Mansfield; Professor Barbara Lehman, Ph.D., The Ohio State University at Mansfield; Professor Joseph Martinez, Chair of Theatre Department, Washington and Lee University; Shelly Minck, Lowell Radke, Rodger Smith, Tammy Smith, Marna Utz, Art & Sylvia Weiss, Helen Wenzel, Tony Woodard, my endlessly supportive mother, Ann Foster; my most precious and beautiful children, Dylan, Sanya & Ian; and my infinitely patient and loving wife, Nellie.

A very special thank you to Professor John Ahart, Ph.D., Head of the MFA Directing Program, The University of Illinois, Champaign–Urbana; Peggy O'Brian, Head of Education, The Folger Shakespeare Library, Washington, D.C.; Christine San Jose, Ph.D., Senior Editor, HIGHLIGHTS FOR CHILDREN; George Wenzel, Computer Specialist, The Ohio State University at Mansfield; Suzan L. Zeder, playwright for children and adult audiences; and my little sister, Linda F. Radke, entrepreneur extraordinaire, who became a publisher to make sure this book would come to be.

Author's Notes

This book is written with two audiences in mind: The adult who wishes to read to the child and the child able to read on his or her own. Those of you reading to or with a child are encouraged to start at an early age. My wife and I read this material to our son, Ian, who is just over a year old. We certainly don't expect him to maintain a lengthy attention span, but we hope we are creating an environment that will develop an interest in reading as well as an expanded vocabulary. The appropriate age for the child reading on his own will vary. Some children will be ten years old before being comfortable with material of this nature, while others will start as early as six.

Shakespeare was a poet in the habit of creating new words. His audiences may not have understood every word spoken but they had no problem following and enjoying his plays. If your children are unable to find some of his words in a dictionary, their wonderfully active imaginations will have no problem filling in the blanks. Do point out to the child that this is an edited version. I hope the interest they develop from this children's edition will inspire them to seek out the complete Shakespeare plays.

At the end of the book there are questions for those who seek guidance in discussing the play. The questions are designed to help the child relate to the story and become even more comfortable in expressing thoughts and feelings. The questions are open-ended so there can be no wrong answers. As parents, or educators, we look for occasions to praise children. These questions are excellent opportunities to praise them for their cleverness, insight, imagination, expanded vocabulary, improved reading skills and ability to express themselves. The most important consideration is that reading (or being read to) be an enjoyable experience. I certainly hope you and the child enjoy what lies ahead.

First edition, 1989.

Back cover photo of author by Jim Hogg

All rights reserved. Printed in the United States of America.

Library of Congress Catalog Card Number: 89-80371

ISBN: 0-961-9853-X
        0-961-9853-5-6 Library Edition

Five Star Publications, P.O. Box 3142, Scottsdale, AZ 85271-3142 (602) 941-0770

0 9 8 7 6 5 4 3 2 1

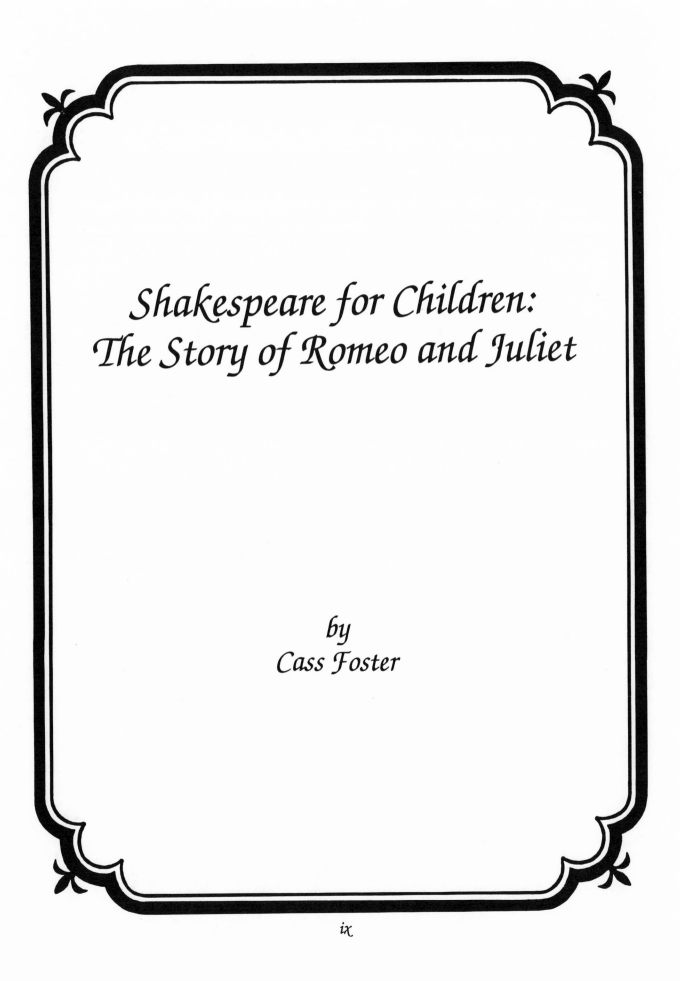

Shakespeare for Children:
The Story of Romeo and Juliet

by
Cass Foster

*W*elcome to the enchanted world of the Bard, William Shakespeare. A world that often includes cunning Kings & Queens, noble knights, wicked witches, clever clowns and mysterious magicians.

*S*hakespeare was born in Stratford-upon-Avon over four hundred years ago when Queen Elizabeth I ruled England. He wrote thirty-seven plays and is considered by many to be the greatest playwright to ever live.

Let us sit back and enjoy his brilliance and genius as we enter a world that promises timeless and unforgettable adventures.

William Shakespeare
1564 - 1616

Contents

Cast of Characters

ESCALUS, Prince of Verona
PARIS, A young nobleman, kinsman to the Prince
FRIAR LAURENCE, A Franciscan
FRIAR JOHN, A Franciscan
APOTHECARY
THREE MUSICIANS
AN OFFICER OF THE PRINCE

MONTAGUES:

MONTAGUE, Head of the household
ROMEO, Son to Montague
MERCUTIO, Friend of Romeo, kinsman of the prince
BENVOLIO, Friend of Romeo, nephew to Montague
BALTHASAR, Servant to Romeo
ABRAM, Servant to Montague
LADY MONTAGUE, Wife of Montague

CAPULETS:

CAPULET, Head of the household
TYBALT, Nephew to Lady Capulet
GREGORY, Servant to Capulet
SAMPSON, Servant to Capulet
PETER, Servant to Juliet's nurse
LADY CAPULET, Wife of Capulet
JULIET, Daughter of Capulet
NURSE, Nanny to Juliet

LOCATIONS:
Verona and Mantua

TIME:
Fourteenth Century

thus begins

our first act

of

The Tragedy of
Romeo and Juliet

Prologue

We start our journey in the ancient city of Verona, where we can expect to see beautiful stone houses, busy market places, lush, green hillsides, abundant lakes and streams and children laughing and playing. The setting is disturbed as the prologue reveals:

Two households, both alike in dignity[1],
In fair Verona, where we lay our scene,
From ancient grudge, break to new mutiny[2],
Where civil blood makes civil hands unclean:
From forth the fatal loins of these two foes,
A pair of star-crossed[3] lovers take their life;
Whose misadventured piteous overthrows,
Doth with their death bury their parent's strife.

1. DIGNITY .... social position
2. MUTINY .... discord
3. STAR-CROSSED .... ill-fated

"A PAIR OF STAR-CROSSED LOVERS."

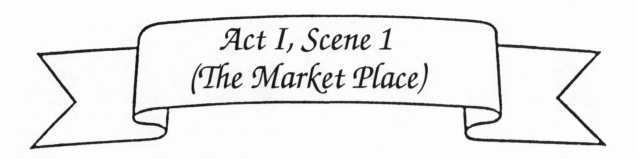

Act I, Scene 1
(The Market Place)

The play begins in a noisy and crowded market place. Peddlers sell fruits and vegetables, bolts of cloth, hand-made brooms and anything else the residents of Verona might need. A number of young Capulets come across a band of proud Montagues. The two families have been feuding for years and it doesn't take long before they draw their rapiers and begin fighting. Many on each side are seriously hurt as the Prince enters:

PRINCE   Rebellious subjects, enemies to peace,
You men, you beasts, on pain of torture
Throw your mistempered[1] weapons to the ground
And hear the sentence of your moved[2] Prince:

All the men lay their rapiers on the ground, fearful of what the Prince will say:

PRINCE   If ever you disturb our streets again,
Your lives shall pay the forfeit of the peace.
You, Capulet, shall go along with me, and,
Montague, come you this afternoon, to know our
Farther pleasure in this case. Once more, on pain
Of death, all men depart.

The Capulets and Montagues depart in different directions. They do not turn their backs on each other for fear of what the others might do.

1. MISTEMPERED ....made for an evil purpose
2. MOVED ....angry

"REBELLIOUS SUBJECTS, ENEMIES TO PEACE."

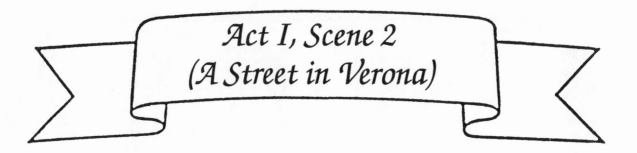

Act I, Scene 2
(A Street in Verona)

On a quiet cobblestone street in Verona, Romeo and his friends come across a servant of Capulet. The servant is carrying an invitation list to a Capulet party. Since the servant cannot read, he asks Romeo to read the list:

ROMEO   A fair assembly: whither should they come?

SERVANT   To supper, to our house.

ROMEO   Whose house?

SERVANT   My master's.

ROMEO   Indeed, I should have asked you that before.

SERVANT   My master is the great rich Capulet;
If you be not of the House of Montague,
I pray come and crush[1] a cup of wine.

Romeo and his friends are Montagues but since everyone at the party will be wearing masks, they decide to attend. They agree to pick up their masks at home and meet on a road near the Capulets.

1.   CRUSH ....drink

"A FAIR ASSEMBLY:
WHITHER SHOULD THEY COME?"

Act I, Scene 3
(Capulet's House)

The Capulets are a wealthy family and their home is richly decorated. As we enter the Capulet's sitting room we discover that Lady Capulet would like Juliet to marry Paris—a young man Juliet has never met:

LADY CAPULET   Tell me, daughter Juliet,
How stands your disposition to be married?

JULIET   It is an honor that I dream not of.

LADY CAPULET   Well think of marriage now. Younger than you,
Here in Verona, ladies of esteem,
Are made already mothers. By my count,
I was your mother[1] much upon these years
That you are now a maid. Thus then in brief:
The gallant Paris seeks you for his love,
What say you? Can you love the gentleman?[2]
This night you shall behold him at our feast.

JULIET   I'll look to like, if looking liking move.[3]

---

1. I WAS YOUR MOTHER ....Lady Capulet was fourteen when she gave birth to Juliet.

2. CAN YOU LOVE THIS GENTLEMAN? ....It was common practice in Elizabethan England for parents to arrange marriages. That doesn't mean the child always wanted to go along with the idea.

3. I'LL LOOK TO LIKE ....Juliet is prepared to look favorably on Paris.

"HOW STANDS YOUR
DISPOSITION TO BE MARRIED?"

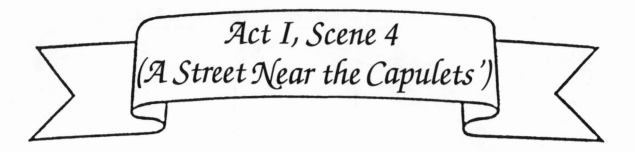

Act I, Scene 4
(A Street Near the Capulets')

Romeo and his friends are on their way to the Capulet party. Benvolio and Mercutio tell Romeo they are looking forward to seeing him dance at the party:

ROMEO   Not I, believe me; you have dancing shoes
With nimble soles; I have a soul of lead
So stakes me to the ground I cannot move.

Mercutio is always clowning around. He puts his arm around Romeo and teases him:

MERCUTIO   You are a lover. Borrow Cupid's wings and
Soar with them above a common bound.[1]

They all laugh as they walk to the Capulets.

---

1.   BOUND .... leap. Many dances at this time had leaping steps.

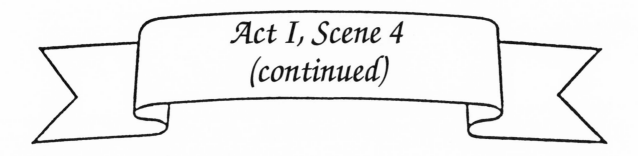

In the midst of their joking Romeo stops as he remembers a disturbing dream he had the night before:

ROMEO And we mean well in going to this masque;[1]
But 'tis no wit[2] to go.

MERCUTIO Why, may one ask?

ROMEO I dream'd a dream tonight…

BENVOLIO Supper is done and we shall come too late!

ROMEO I fear too early; for my mind misgives
Some consequence[3] yet hanging in the stars,
Shall bitterly begin his fearful date
With this night's revels and expire the term
Of a despised life, closed in my breast,
By some vile forfeit of untimely death.

Romeo is not happy with the idea but he joins his friends as they continue their walk to the party.

1. MASQUE ....masquerade party

2. NO WIT..not wise

3. CONSEQUENCE..............................event to come

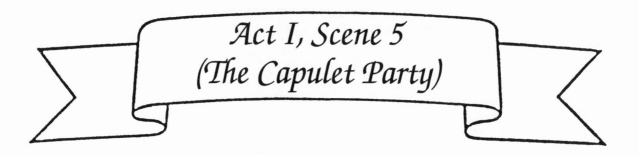

Act I, Scene 5
(The Capulet Party)

Romeo and his friends join the festivities and discover the Capulets have a beautiful and spacious home. All the guests are well dressed and wearing fancy masks.

There is merriment everywhere as couples dance to the sounds of flutes and stringed instruments. The graceful and popular Juliet is asked to dance by many handsome young knights. Romeo notices Juliet:

ROMEO   What lady's that, which doth enrich the hand
Of yonder knight?

SERVANT   I know not sir.

ROMEO   O, she doth teach the torches to burn bright!
For I ne'er saw true beauty will this night!

Romeo can feel his heart pounding. It takes all the courage he can find but he manages to ask Juliet to dance.

"I NE'ER SAW TRUE BEAUTY TILL THIS NIGHT!"

Tybalt recognizes Romeo and cannot believe a Montague would dare enter the House of Capulet:

TYBALT   This, by his voice, should be a Montague.
Fetch me my rapier, boy.

CAPULET   Why, how now kinsman? Wherefore storm you so?

TYBALT   Uncle, this is a Montague, our foe!

CAPULET   Young Romeo is it?

TYBALT   'Tis he, that villain Romeo!

CAPULET   Content thee, gentle cuz[1], let him alone.
And, to say truth, Verona brags of him
To be a virtuous and well-governed[2] youth.

TYBALT   I'll not endure him.

CAPULET   He shall be endured!
Am I the master here, or you? Go to!

TYBALT   I will withdraw: but this intrusion shall,
Now seeming sweet, convert to bitter gall.

Tybalt angrily withdraws!

1. CUZ ....Capulet is Tybalt's uncle but Elizabethans used the term
cousin for most relatives other than parent or brother and sister.

2. WELL-GOVERNED ....well behaved

"UNCLE, THIS IS A MONTAGUE, OUR FOE!"

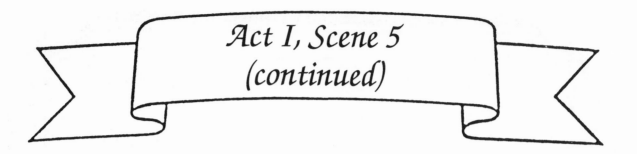

Romeo and Juliet see and hear only each other. The longer they dance, the more they feel they have known one other all their lives. Their hands are joined as they slowly stop dancing:

ROMEO   O then, dear saint, let lips do what hands do!
They pray. Grant thou, lest faith turn to despair.

JULIET   Saints do not move, though grant for prayer's sake.

ROMEO   Then move not, while my prayer's effect I take.

Romeo slowly reaches out to Juliet and tenderly kisses her lips.

"LET LIPS DO WHAT HANDS DO!"

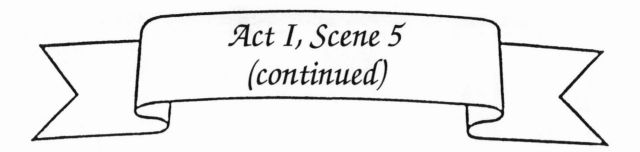

The tenderness of the moment is broken as the Nurse enters:

NURSE   Madam, your mother craves a word with you.

Juliet exits looking at Romeo the entire time. Once Juliet is out of sight Romeo asks:

ROMEO   Who is her mother?

NURSE   Marry Bachelor,
Her mother is the lady of the house.

ROMEO   Is she a Capulet?
O dear account! My life is my foe's debt.[1]

Romeo is confused and quickly leaves the party.

1.   MY FOE'S DEBT ....I am no longer free. My heart belongs to Juliet.

"HER MOTHER IS THE LADY OF THE HOUSE."

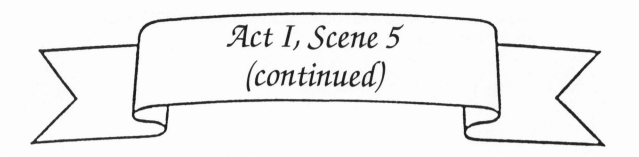

Juliet returns and discovers Romeo has left. She never did learn his name so she asks her Nurse who he is:

NURSE   His name is Romeo, and a Montague,
The only son of your great enemy.

JULIET   My only love, sprung from my only hate!
Too early seen unknown, and known too late!
Prodigious[1] birth of love it is to me
That I must love a loathed enemy.

Juliet, like Romeo, is terribly confused. Her parents want her to marry a man she has never met and here she is, falling in love with the son of her father's worst enemy. Without drawing any attention to herself, Juliet quietly withdraws to her room.

1. PRODIGIOUS .... ominous

"THE ONLY SON OF YOUR GREAT ENEMY."

Thus ends
the first act of

Romeo and Juliet

Act II

of

Romeo and Juliet

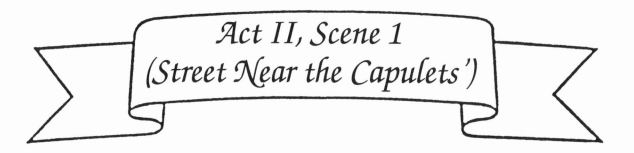

Act II, Scene 1
(Street Near the Capulets')

The Capulet party is over and Romeo's friends are outside looking for him. Even though Romeo knows it would be a mistake to fall in love with a Capulet, is unable to pull himself away from Juliet's house. Romeo hides from his friends when he hears them calling:

BENVOLIO   Romeo! My cousin Romeo! Romeo!

MERCUTIO   He is wise,
And on my life, hath stol'n him home to bed.

BENVOLIO   He ran this way, and leapt this orchard wall.
Come, he hath hid himself among these trees.

MERCUTIO   'Tis in vain
To seek him here that means not to be found

Benvolio and Mercutio return home without the lovestruck Romeo.

"'TIS IN VAIN TO SEEK HIM."

Act II, Scene 2
(Beneath Juliet's Balcony)

It is late. The moon shines bright as Romeo sits beneath a tree thinking of the beautiful young woman who so unexpectedly entered his life. Much to Romeo's surprise, Juliet appears on the balcony of her room but does not see him:

ROMEO   But soft! What light through yonder window breaks?
It is the East, and Juliet is the sun!
It is my lady, O, it is my love!
O that she knew she were!
See how she leans her cheek upon her hand!
O that I were a glove upon that hand,
That I might touch that cheek!

"WHAT LIGHT THROUGH
YONDER WINDOW BREAKS?"

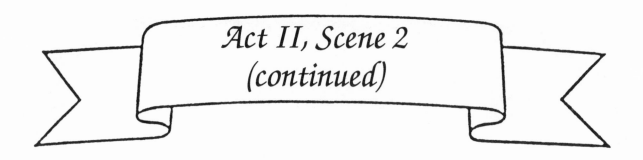

Juliet is still unaware of Romeo's presence. Her face is softly lit by the pale moon and a gentle breeze passes through her golden hair as she wonders aloud:

JULIET   O Romeo, Romeo! Wherefore art thou Romeo?
Deny thy father and refuse thy name.
'Tis but thy name that is my enemy.
What's in a name? That which we call a rose
By any other name would smell as sweet.

ROMEO   I know not how to tell thee who I am.
My name, dear saint, is hateful to myself,
Because it is an enemy to thee.

Juliet is startled when she thinks she recognizes Romeo's voice:

JULIET   My ears have not yet drunk a hundred words
Of that tongue's uttering, yet I know the sound.

Juliet looks down.

JULIET   Art thou not Romeo and a Montague?

ROMEO   Neither, fair maid, if either thee dislike.

"O ROMEO, ROMEO!
WHEREFORE ART THOU ROMEO?"

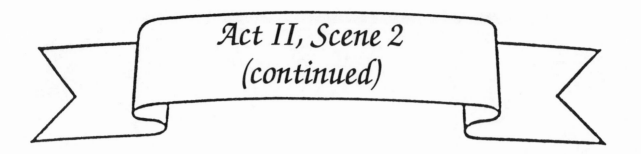

Act II, Scene 2
(continued)

Romeo can no longer contain himself. He leaps upon the balcony!
Juliet is both startled and star-struck:

JULIET   If they do see thee, they will murder thee.

ROMEO   I have night's cloak to hide me from their eyes:
And but thou love me, let them find me here.

JULIET   O gentle Romeo,
If thou dost love, pronounce it faithfully.

ROMEO   O blessed, blessed night! I am afeared,
Being in night, all this is but a dream.

JULIET   If that thy bent of love be honorable,
Thy purpose marriage, send me word tomorrow.

"THEY WILL MURDER THEE."

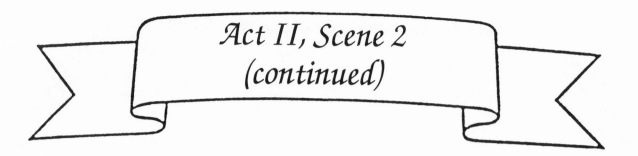

Act II, Scene 2
(continued)

Romeo starts to climb down from the balcony as Juliet reaches to him:

JULIET   Good night, good night! Parting is such sweet sorrow.

The sadness in Juliet's eyes makes it impossible for Romeo to leave. He climbs back up the balcony and stays with Juliet until the sun begins to rise and he knows he must go:

ROMEO   Sleep dwell upon thine eyes, peace in thy breast.
Would I were sleep and peace, so sweet to rest.
Hence will I to my ghostly[1] father's cell,
His help to crave and my dear hap[2] to tell.

1.   GHOSTLY ....spiritual

2.   DEAR HAP ....the happy fortune that has befallen me

"PARTING IS SUCH SWEET SORROW."

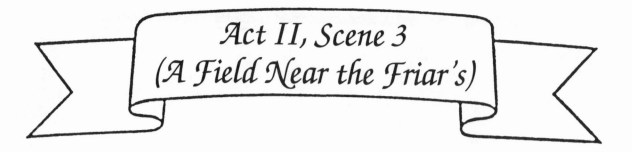

Act II, Scene 3
(A Field Near the Friar's)

The Friar has completed his morning prayers and is in the field gathering herbs and wild flowers. The herbs will be used for healing and the flowers will add a sweet fragrance to his humble home. The Friar is enjoying the start of another day as his young friend, Romeo, approaches:

FRIAR   Our Romeo hath not been in bed tonight.

ROMEO   That is true, the sweeter rest was mine.
                I have been feasting with mine enemy.

FRIAR   Be plain good son, and homely in thy drift.

ROMEO   Than plainly know my heart's dear love is set
                On the fair daughter of rich Capulet. But this I
                Pray, that thou consent to marry us today.

FRIAR   Holy Saint Francis! What a change is here!

The good Friar agrees for one reason:

FRIAR   In one respect I'll thy assistant be;
                For this alliance may so happy prove
                To turn your households' rancor to pure love.

"TURN YOUR HOUSEHOLDS'
RANCOR TO PURE LOVE."

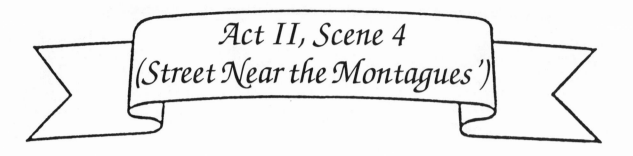

Act II, Scene 4
(Street Near the Montagues')

Later that day Juliet sent her Nurse to learn of Romeo's intentions. The Nurse is accompanied by Peter, a Capulet servant, as they come across Romeo and his friends:

ROMEO   Here's a goodly gear![1]

MERCUTIO   A sail, a sail![2]

NURSE   Peter!

PETER   Anon![3]

NURSE   My fan, Peter.

MERCUTIO   Good Peter, to hide her face: for the fan's the
               Fairer of the two.

Mercutio doesn't mean any harm when he teases the Nurse but she does not appreciate being laughed at. The Nurse pulls Romeo away from his friends to learn of his intentions towards Juliet:

1. GOODLY GEAR ....this ought to be fun

2. A SAIL, A SAIL! ....the call of sailors on seeing a ship on the horizon

3. ANON ....I'm coming

"A SAIL, A SAIL!"

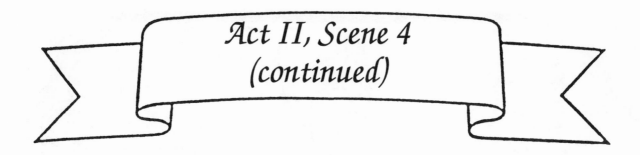

Romeo carefully explains the plan to the Nurse:

ROMEO   Bid her devise
Some means to come to shrift[1] this afternoon;
And there she shall at Friar Laurence's cell
Be shrived[2] and married.

Romeo hands the Nurse a coin for her troubles. She curtsies out
of appreciation and begins her long walk back to Juliet.

1. SHRIFT .... confession
2. SHRIVED .... absolved from sin

"BID HER DEVISE
SOME MEANS TO COME TO SHRIFT."

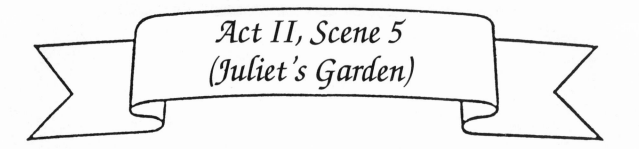

Act II, Scene 5
(Juliet's Garden)

Juliet is in her garden, surrounded by marble statues, beautiful fountains and fresh-smelling flowers. She sits impatiently, awaiting the Nurse's return. The Nurse finally shows up but takes forever to tell Juliet of Romeo's intentions:

NURSE   I am aweary, give my leave awhile.

JULIET   Nay, come, I pray thee speak. Good, good Nurse, speak.

NURSE   Jesu, what haste! Can you not stay awhile?
Do you not see that I am out of breath?

JULIET   How are thou out of breath when thou hast
Breath to say to me that thou are out of breath?

NURSE   Lord, how my head aches! What a head have I!
It beats as it would fall in twenty pieces.

Juliet rubs the Nurse's head:

JULIET   I' faith, I am sorry that thou are not well.
Sweet, sweet, sweet Nurse, tell me, what says my love?

"SWEET, SWEET, SWEET NURSE,
TELL ME, WHAT SAYS MY LOVE?"

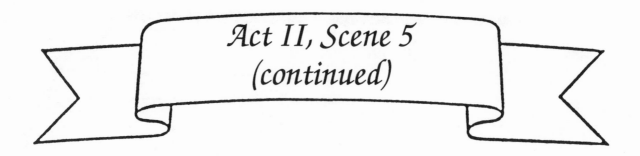

The Nurse finally explains the plan:

NURSE   Have you got leave to go to shrift today?

JULIET   I have.

NURSE   Then hie[1] you hence to Friar Laurence's cell,
There stays a husband to make you a wife.
Go; I'll to dinner, hie you to the cell.

Juliet is ecstatic!

JULIET   Hie to high fortune! Honest Nurse, farewell!

Juliet exits.

---

1.   HIE .... hurry

"THERE STAYS A HUSBAND
TO MAKE YOU A WIFE."

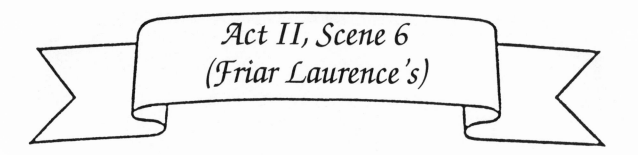

Act II, Scene 6
(Friar Laurence's)

The Friar's cell, unlike Juliet's home, is simply furnished and very small. Juliet is quick to meet Romeo and the Friar is amused at how excited and child-like the two young lovers are:

FRIAR   Come, come with me, and we will make short work;
For, by your leaves, holy church shall incorporate
Two in one.

Romeo and Juliet join the Friar at the Altar. They slowly kneel before him as they repeat the sacred vows that unite them as man and wife.

"HOLY CHURCH SHALL
INCORPORATE TWO IN ONE."

*T*he wedding of Romeo and Juliet brings Act II to a close. If our play were to stop here, all would be well, but Shakespeare meant for us to see what terrible consequences could come from two families that only know violence as a means to settle differences.

Act III

of

Romeo and Juliet

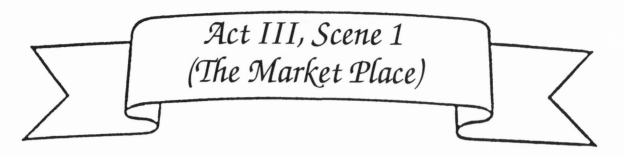

Act III, Scene 1
(The Market Place)

The market is very busy with vendors selling their wares and friends visiting each other. Tybalt enters at one end of the market and notices Romeo at the other end. Tybalt has been waiting for an opportunity to draw Romeo into a fight. Romeo is so much in love, he is willing to ignore Tybalt's insults:

TYBALT   Thou art a villain. Therefore turn and draw.

ROMEO   I do protest I never injured thee
                 But love thee better than thou canst devise.[1]

Tybalt doesn't realize that he and Romeo are now cousins. In the meantime, Mercutio draws his rapier and challenges Tybalt, a master swordsman:

MERCUTIO   Tybalt, you ratcatcher, will you walk?[2]

TYBALT   What wouldst thou have with me?

MERCUTIO   Good king of cats, nothing but one of your nine lives.

TYBALT   I am for you!

Tybalt loves the thought of embarrassing Mercutio in front of all his friends so he draws his sword and they fight.

At first Tybalt demonstrates his superiority as a master swordsman but after awhile Mercutio proves to be the better. Tybalt is humiliated and begins to fight more angrily. The fight is getting out of hand and Romeo reminds them of the Prince's order.

---

1.   DEVISE .... imagine

2.   WALK .... step aside a moment

"TYBALT, YOU RATCATCHER, WILL YOU WALK?"

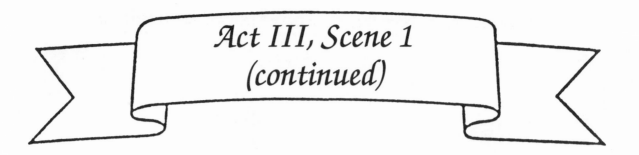

Romeo realizes Tybalt and Mercutio could easily do each other great harm so he quickly grabs hold of Mercutio. Just as Mercutio is being pulled away, Tybalt accidentally thrusts his rapier into him. Romeo is unaware that Mercutio has been stabbed as Tybalt and his friends quickly depart:

MERCUTIO   I am hurt!
A plague o' both your houses!

ROMEO   Courage, man. The hurt cannot be much.

MERCUTIO   No, 'tis not so deep as a well, nor so wide
As a church door: but 'tis enough, 'twill serve.
Ask for me tomorrow, and you shall find me a
Grave man. Why the devil came you between us?

ROMEO   I thought all for the best.

MERCUTIO   I was hurt under your arm! Help me into some
House, Benvolio or I shall faint. A plague o' both
Your houses! I am sped.[1]

Mercutio drops his rapier as he collapses. Benvolio helps him up and carries him to a physician.

---

1. SPED ....destroyed

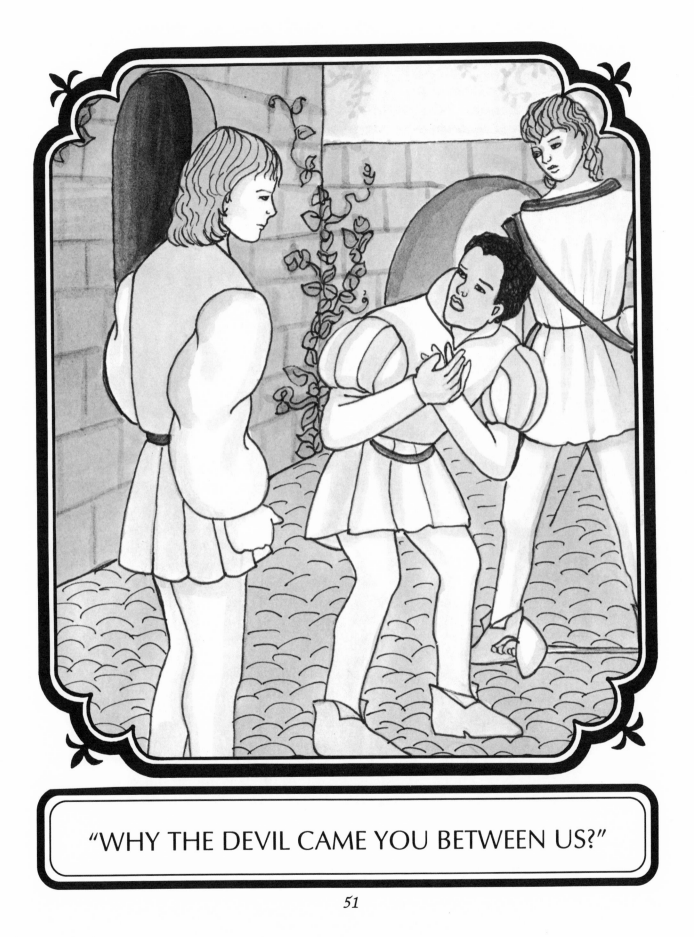

"WHY THE DEVIL CAME YOU BETWEEN US?"

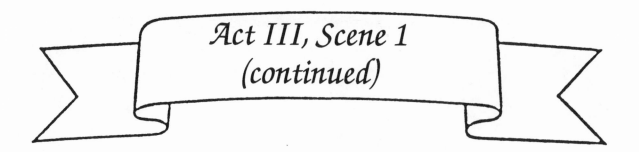

Romeo is left alone, feeling responsible for Mercutio's wound:

ROMEO   My very friend, hath got his mortal hurt
On my behalf...O, sweet Juliet,
Thy beauty hath made me effeminate.[1]

Benvolio returns in tears and finds it very difficult to speak:

BENVOLIO   O Romeo, Romeo, brave Mercutio's dead!

Tybalt returns. He still wants to fight with Romeo. Romeo is furious and can no longer contain himself:

ROMEO   Alive in triumph, and Mercutio slain?
Mercutio's soul is but a little way above our heads,
Staying for thine to keep him company.
Either thou, or I, or both must go with him.

Romeo picks up Mercutio's rapier and they fight furiously. Their fight leads them all over the market place. They knock down a number of food carts as fearful parents push their children out of the way. Tybalt has Romeo on the ground and is about to stab him when Romeo quickly turns over and thrusts his rapier into Tybalt. Romeo flees quickly, once he realizes what he has done.

1.   EFFEMINATE ....soft, unwilling to fight

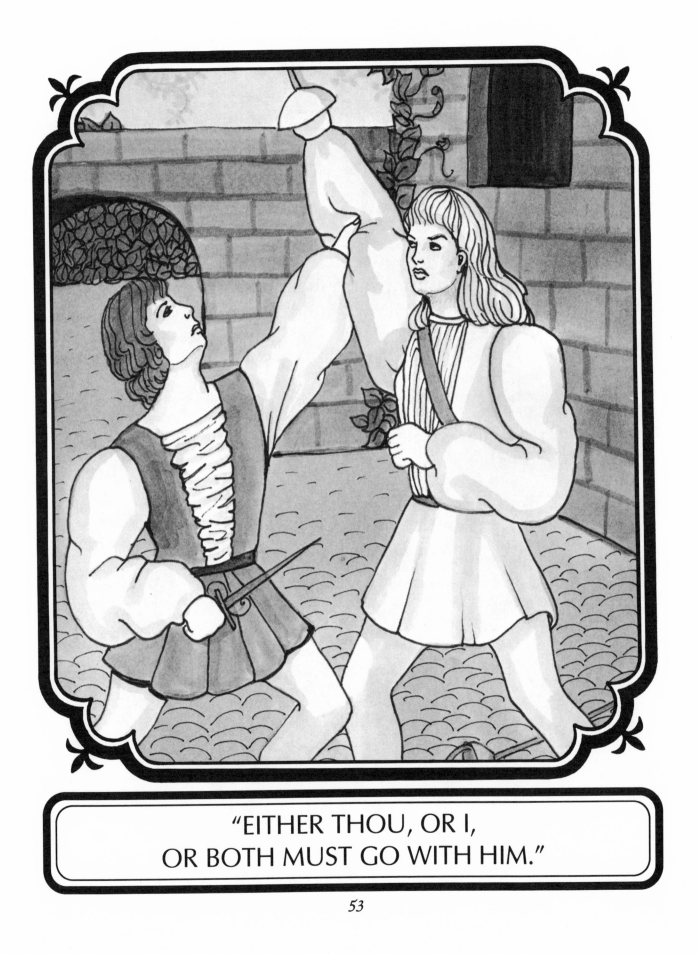

"EITHER THOU, OR I,
OR BOTH MUST GO WITH HIM."

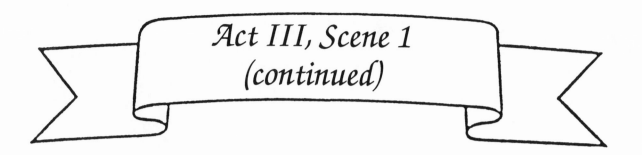

The Prince arrives and the Capulets demand Romeo be put to death:

LADY CAPULET   I beg for justice, which thou, Prince, must give.
Romeo slew Tybalt: Romeo must not live.

Montague reminds the Prince that Tybalt killed Mercutio:

MONTAGUE   Not Romeo, Prince; he was Mercutio's friend;
His fault concludes but what the law should end,
The life of Tybalt.

PRINCE   And for that offense
Immediately we do exile[1] him hence,
Else, when he is found, that hour is his last.

---

1.   EXILE .... Romeo is to leave Verona and never see his family again.

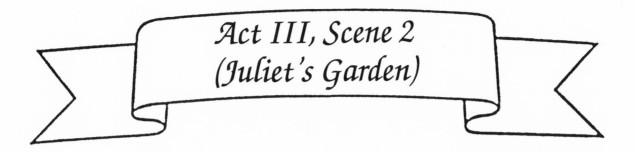

Act III, Scene 2
(Juliet's Garden)

Juliet is walking through her garden, enjoying her flowers and the peace and quiet. The Nurse arrives with the terrible news:

NURSE   Ah, well-a-day! He's dead, he's dead, he's dead!

JULIET   What devil art thou that dost torment me thus?
             Hath Romeo slain himself?

NURSE   Oh Tybalt, Tybalt, the best friend I had!
             That ever I should live to see thee dead!

JULIET   Is Romeo slaughtered and is Tybalt dead?
             My dearest cousin, and my dearer lord?

NURSE   Tybalt is gone, and Romeo banished;
             Romeo that killed him, he is banished.

JULIET   O God! Did Romeo's hand shed Tybalt's blood?

NURSE   It did, it did! Alas the day, it did!

JULIET   O serpent heart, hid with a flow'ring face!
             Did ever dragon keep so fair a cave?
             Was ever book containing such vile matter
             So fairly bound? O, that deceit should dwell
             In such a gorgeous palace!

Juliet is in a state of shock. The Nurse offers to find Romeo and ask him to come to Juliet before he leaves the country.

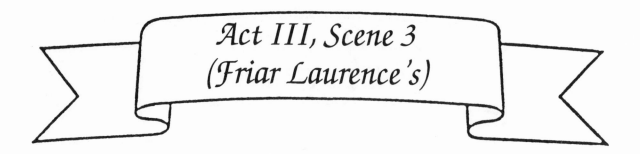

Act III, Scene 3
(Friar Laurence's)

We return to the austere cell of Friar Laurence, where Romeo has been waiting to learn of the Prince's order:

ROMEO   Rather, what news? What is the Prince's doom?

FRIAR   Not body's death, but body's banishment.

ROMEO   Ha, banishment? Be merciful, say "death";
              For exile hath more terror in his look.

The Friar reminds Romeo how fortunate he is:

FRIAR   But the kind Prince,
              Taking thy part, that rush'd aside the law,
              And turned that black word, death, to banishment.
              This is dear mercy, and thou seest it not.

The Nurse enters and tells Romeo that Juliet is in desperate need of him.

"THIS IS DEAR MERCY."

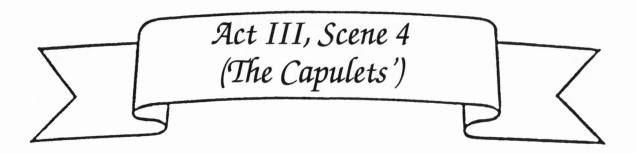

Act III, Scene 4
('The Capulets')

Paris suggests that his marriage to Juliet be delayed in order to properly mourn the loss of Tybalt:

PARIS   These times of woe afford no time to woo.

Capulet thinks the wedding will help take Juliet's mind off her sorrow. Out of respect for Tybalt, he will keep the ceremony simple:

CAPULET   We'll keep no great ado; a friend or two;
For hark you, Tybalt being slain so late,
It may be thought we held him carelessly,
Being our kinsmen, if we revel much.

"THESE TIMES OF WOE
AFFORD NO TIME TO WOO."

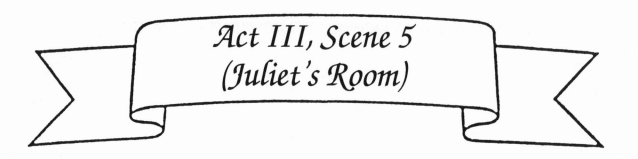

Act III, Scene 5
(Juliet's Room)

Romeo is now with his fair Juliet. Our two young lovers are finally able to spend a night together as man and wife. Romeo must leave before daylight or risk execution at the hands of the Prince. The sound of a lark will warn our troubled couple the sun is about to rise.

As the two of them lie comfortably and securely in each other's arms, Romeo thinks he hears the sound of a lark and starts to get out of bed:

JULIET   Wilt thou be gone? It is not yet near day.
It was the Nightingale, and not the Lark,
That pierced the fearful hollow of thine ear,
Believe me, love, it was the Nightingale.

The singing of the Lark can be heard:

ROMEO   It was the Lark, the herald of the morn,
I must be gone and live or stay and die.

"I MUST BE GONE AND LIVE, OR STAY AND DIE."

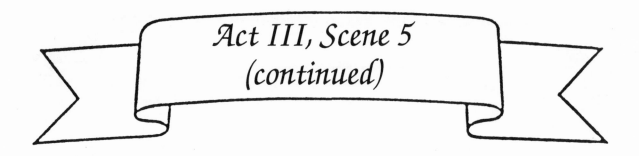

The Nurse enters hastily, practically out of breath:

NURSE   Your lady mother is coming to your chamber.
                   The day is broke: be wary, look about.

The Nurse exits and Juliet realizes Romeo must depart:

JULIET   Then, window, let day in, and let life out.

ROMEO   Farewell, farewell! One kiss and I'll descend.

They kiss and Romeo is about to climb down the balcony as Juliet
desperately reaches to him:

JULIET   O, think'st thou we shall ever meet again?

Romeo does his best to reassure Juliet:

ROMEO   I doubt it not; adieu! Adieu!

Romeo quickly departs for Mantua but Juliet is not at all reassured:

JULIET   O God, I have an ill-diving soul!

"ONE KISS AND I'LL DESCEND."

Act III, Scene 1
(continued)

Lady Capulet enters to tell Juliet of the wedding plans. Juliet has completely forgotten that her parents want her to marry Paris. They don't realize she is already married to Romeo:

LADY CAPULET   Why, how now, Juliet?

JULIET   Madam, I am not well.

LADY CAPULET   But now, I'll tell thee joyful tidings, girl.

JULIET   And joy comes well in such a needy time.

LADY CAPULET   Marry, my child, early next Thursday morn
The gallant, young, and noble gentleman,
The County[1] Paris, at Saint Peter's Church,
Shall happily make thee there a joyful bride.

JULIET   I pray you, tell my lord and father, madam,
I will not marry yet: and when I do, I swear
It shall be Romeo, whom you know I hate,
Rather than Paris. These are news indeed!

LADY CAPULET   Here comes your father. Tell him so yourself!

Capulet enters and makes it clear he doesn't want to see his daughter again, should she refuse to marry Paris. Juliet decides if anyone has a solution to this problem it will be Friar Laurence. Act III comes to a close with Juliet leaving for the Friar's cell.

1. COUNTY .... Count or Earl

"MADAM, I AM NOT WELL."

Act IV
of
Romeo and Juliet

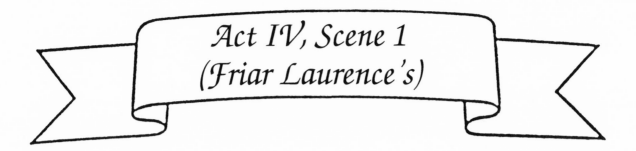

Act IV, Scene 1
(Friar Laurence's)

The Friar is alone in his quiet cell, just completing his afternoon prayers, when Juliet arrives.   By now she is feeling terribly depressed. She has given up all hope of ever seeing Romeo again:

JULIET   Come weep with me; past hope, past cure, past help!

FRIAR   Hold daughter, I do spy a kind of hope.
                    And, if thou darest, I'll give thee remedy.

The Friar has a plan and Juliet's hopes are renewed:

JULIET   And, will do it without fear or doubt,
                    To live an unstained wife to my sweet love.

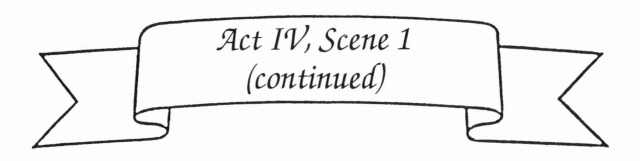

The Friar offers Juliet a drug that will make it appear she has died:

FRIAR
Hold then, go home, be merry, give consent
To marry Paris. Wednesday is tomorrow.
Tomorrow night look that thou lie alone.
Let not thy nurse lie with thee in thy chamber.
Take thou this vial, being then in bed,
When presently through all the veins shall run
No warmth, nor breath, shall testify thou livest:
Thou shalt continue two and forty hours,
And then awake as from a pleasant sleep.

Juliet knew she could rely on the good Friar. She agrees to the plan and the Friar explains he will send a messenger to Mantua to tell Romeo of their scheme.

"TAKE THOU THIS VIAL."

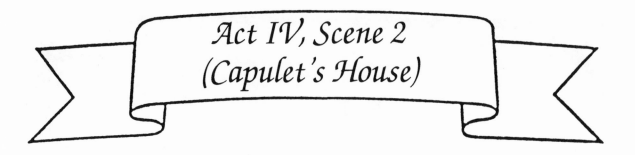

Act IV, Scene 2
(Capulet's House)

Juliet immediately returns home. She finds her father in his study and pretends to look forward to her marriage to Paris. Lord Capulet can hardly believe her change of heart:

CAPULET   Well, I will walk myself
To County Paris to prepare him up[1] against
Tomorrow. My heart is wondrous light,
Since this same wayward girl is so reclaimed.

1.   PREPARE HIM UP .... tell him to be prepared

"MY HEART IS WONDROUS LIGHT."

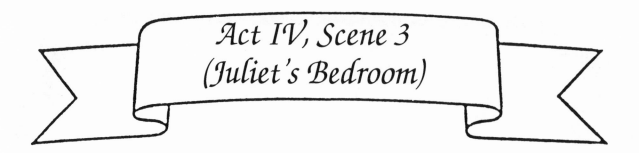

Act IV, Scene 3
(Juliet's Bedroom)

Juliet is ready to take the drug but it seems as if her mother and the Nurse are never going to leave her room:

JULIET   So please you, let me now be left alone,
For I am sure you have your hands full all
In this so sudden business.

LADY   Good night.
CAPULET Get thee to bed and rest, for thou hast need.

The Nurse and Lady Capulet exit. Juliet quietly whispers to herself:

JULIET   Farewell. God knows when we shall meet again.

"LET ME NOW BE LEFT ALONE."

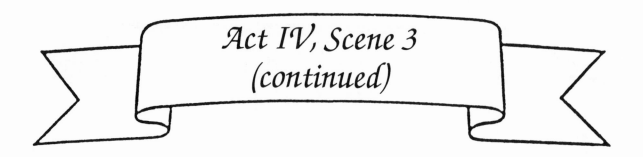

When Juliet was with the Friar, she was full of courage—
now she is filled with doubt:

JULIET   I have a faint cold fear thrills though my veins
That almost freezes up the heat of life.
What if this mixture do not work at all?
Shall I be married then tomorrow morning?
No, no; this shall forbid it. Lie thou there.

Juliet lays a small dagger beside herself. She fills her thoughts with
her beloved Romeo and finds the courage she is lacking:

JULIET   Romeo, I come! This do I drink to thee.

Juliet drinks and crawls into bed.

"ROMEO, I COME! THIS DO I DRINK TO THEE."

Act IV, Scene 4
(Capulet's House)

It is the morning of the wedding and everyone is busy with preparations. They think Juliet is still asleep:

LADY CAPULET

Hold, take these keys and fetch more spices, Nurse.

NURSE

They call for dates and quinces in the pastry.

Capulet enters with all the excitement of a father about to see his only daughter married.

He says to the Nurse:

CAPULET

Go waken Juliet: go and trim her up.[1]
I'll go and chat with Paris. Hie, make haste,
Make haste! The bridegroom he is come already:
Make haste, I say!

The Nurse hurries to Juliet's room.

1.   TRIM HER UP .... help her get ready

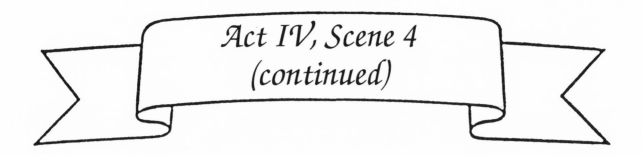

The Nurse enters, eager to help Juliet get ready for the wedding:

NURSE   Mistress! What, mistress! Juliet! Why, lamb! Why, lady! How sound is she asleep! I needs must wake her.

The Nurse gently pushes Juliet and discovers she is cold and lifeless. The Nurse screams!

Lady Capulet rushes into the room:

LADY CAPULET   What noise is here?

NURSE   O lamentable day!

LADY CAPULET   What is the matter?

NURSE   Look, look! O heavy day!

LADY CAPULET   O me, O me! My child, my only life! Revive, look up, or I will die with thee! Help, help! Call help!

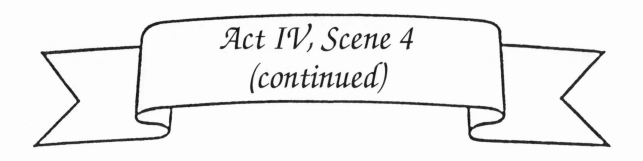

Enter Lord Capulet, upset because Juliet is still in bed:

CAPULET   For shame, bring Juliet forth. Her lord is come.

NURSE   She's dead, deceased. She's dead! Alack the day!

CAPULET   Ha! Let me see her. Out, alas! She's cold,
Her blood is settled, and her joints are stiff.
Life and these lips have long been separated.
Death lies on her like an untimely frost,
Upon the sweetest flower of the field.

Act IV ends as the Capulets' joyful wedding plans become painful preparations for Juliet's funeral.

"DEATH LIES ON HER LIKE AN UNTIMELY FROST."

Act V
of
Romeo and Juliet

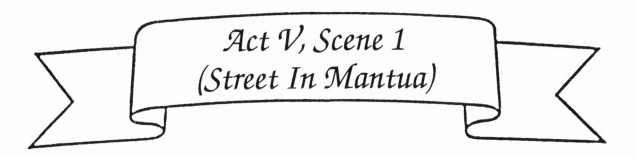

Act V, Scene 1
(Street In Mantua)

Romeo's servant, Balthasar, brings him word of Juliet's death. Romeo has not been told of the Friar's plan and the shocking news leaves him confused and unable to think clearly. He decides his only course of action is to join Juliet in death.

On his way to the Capulet vault (where all members of the Capulet family are entombed) Romeo stops at an Apothecary (pharmacist) to purchase poison:

APOTHECARY   Who calls so loud?

ROMEO   Come hither, man, I see that thou art poor.
Hold, there is forty ducats.[1]
Let me have a dram[2] of poison.

APOTHECARY   Such mortal drugs I have, but Mantua's law
Is death to any he that utters[3] them.

ROMEO   Famine is in thy cheeks.
Need and oppression starveth in thine eyes,
Contempt and beggary hang upon thy back:
The world is not thy friend: nor the world's law;
The world affords no law to make thee rich:
Then be not poor, but break it and take this.

---

1. DUCAT .... gold coin

2. DRAM .... a small amount

3. UTTERS .... sells

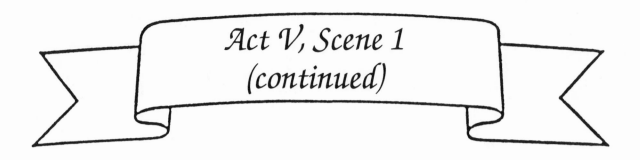

The Apothecary reluctantly agrees to sell Romeo the poison:

APOTHECARY   My poverty, but not my will consents.

ROMEO   There is thy gold, worse poison to men's souls,
Doing more murders in this loathsome world,
Than these poor compounds that thou mayest not sell.

Romeo exchanges his gold for the poison and quickly departs for
the Capulet vault:

"THERE IS THY GOLD,
WORSE POISON TO MEN'S SOULS."

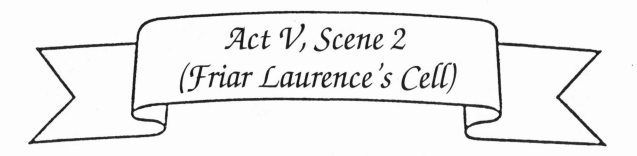

Friar Laurence is relieved to see his messenger return from Mantua. It was the messenger's responsibility to let Romeo know of Juliet's plan to take the drug that will make it appear she has died:

FRIAR LAURENCE

Welcome from Mantua. What says Romeo?

FRIAR JOHN

Because infectious pestilence[1] did reign,
Seal'd up the doors, and would not let us forth,
So that my speed to Mantua was stay'd.[2]

FRIAR LAURENCE

Who bare my letter then to Romeo?

FRIAR JOHN

I could not send it.

FRIAR LAURENCE

Unhappy fortune! The neglecting it
May do much danger.

The Friar is afraid Romeo may get word of Juliet's supposed death. The Friar hurries to the Capulet vault to explain the situation to Romeo.

1. PESTILENCE ....disease
2. STAY'D ....delayed

84

"UNHAPPY FORTUNE!"

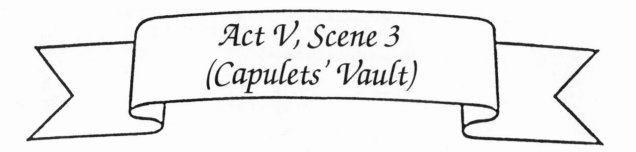

Act V, Scene 3
(Capulets' Vault)

Tybalt and Juliet are laid out on their tombs in the cold, dark and damp Capulet vault. Paris arrives to bid farewell to the woman he had hoped to marry:

PARIS   Sweet flower, with flowers thy bridal bed I strew.
(O woe! Thy canopy[1] is dust and stones)
Which with sweet water[2] nightly I will dew.

Paris is in tears as he covers Juliet with flowers. He hears someone entering the vault and hides in the shadows to see who it is.

1. CANOPY ....sky
2. SWEET WATER ....perfume

"WITH FLOWERS THY BRIDAL BED I STREW."

Act V, Scene 3
(continued)

Romeo's long journey to the Capulet vault is over. He is unable to see how his suicide will only make things worse. As Paris discovers Romeo entering the vault, Paris becomes enraged:

PARIS　　　This is that banished haughty Montague
That murdered my love's cousin—I will apprehend[1] him.
Condemned villain, I do apprehend thee.
Obey, and go with me; for thou must die.

ROMEO　　　I must indeed; and therefore came I hither.
Good gentle youth, tempt not a desp'rate man.
Fly hence and leave me. Think upon these gone;
Put not another sin upon my head
By urging me to fury. O, be gone!

PARIS　　　I do defy thy conjuration[2]
And apprehend thee for a felon here.

ROMEO　　　Wilt thou provoke me?

Paris draws his rapier.

Have at thee, boy!

They fight! Paris, with his long rapier, has the advantage over Romeo, who has a short dagger. Their fight leads them up and down the stairs to the vault. At one point Romeo loses his dagger and is forced to defend himself with a torch. Romeo finally picks up his dagger and as Paris loses his concentration for just a moment, Romeo slays him.

1.　APPREHEND ....arrest

2.　CONJURATION ....warning

88

"I DO DEFY THY CONJURATION."

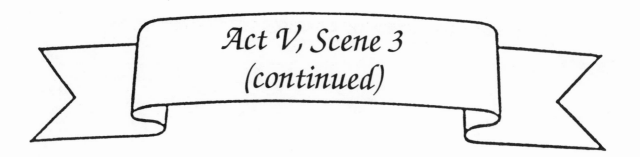

Romeo catches his breath after fighting Paris. It was never Romeo's intention to fight anyone and here he is, responsible for the deaths of two men. Now, lost in his grief, Romeo kneels beside Juliet, preparing to join her:

ROMEO   Eyes, look your last!
Arms, take your last embrace! And, lips, O you
The doors of breath, seal with a righteous kiss
A dateless bargain to engrossing death!
Thou desperate pilot, now at once run on
The dashing rocks thy seasick weary bark!
Here's to my love!

He drinks and the poison takes effect immediately:

ROMEO   True Apothecary!
Thy drugs are quick. Thus with a kiss I die.

Romeo uses his last ounce of strength to kiss Juliet before falling to her side.

"THUS WITH A KISS I DIE."

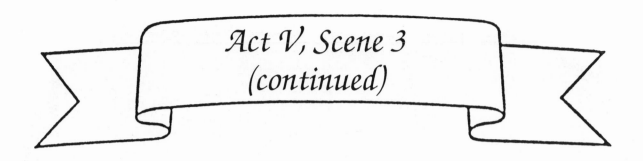

Friar Laurence finally reaches Romeo but he is too late:

FRIAR

Romeo! O, pale! Who else? What, Paris too?
And steep'd in blood? Ah, what an unkind hour
Is guilty of this lamentable chance!

Juliet slowly regains consciousness, realizing how foolish it was to doubt the Friar. The plan worked and now she can hardly wait to see Romeo:

"AH, WHAT AN UNKIND HOUR."

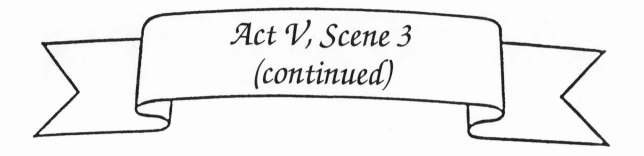

JULIET   O comfortable[1] Friar! Where is my lord?
I do remember well where I should be
And there I am. Where is my Romeo?

FRIAR   I hear some noise. Lady, come from that nest
Of death, contagion, and unnatural sleep.
A greater power than we can contradict
Hath thwarted our intents. Come, come away.
Thy husband in thy bosom there lies dead;
And Paris too. Come, I'll dispose of thee
Among a sisterhood of holy nuns.
Stay not to question, for the watch is coming.
Come, go, good Juliet. I dare no longer stay.

JULIET   Go, get thee hence, for I will not away.

The Friar can hear the Prince about to enter so he quickly runs out,
expecting Juliet to follow.

1.   COMFORTABLE .... helpful

"WHERE IS MY ROMEO?"

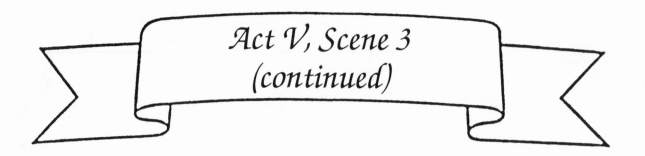

It never occurred to the Friar what a terrible mistake it would be to leave Juliet alone:

JULIET   What's here? A cup clos'd in my true love's hand?
Poison, I see, hath been his timeless end.

Juliet drinks from the vial:

JULIET   O churl![1] Drunk all and left no friendly drop
To help me after? I will kiss thy lips,
Haply[2] some poison yet doth hang on them.

Juliet kisses Romeo but there is no remaining poison. She is startled as she hears the Prince about to enter. Juliet pulls Romeo's dagger from its sheath:

JULIET   Yea, noise? Then I'll be brief. O happy dagger!
This is thy sheath;

She stabs herself and in great pain she utters:

There rest, and let me die.

Juliet falls on Romeo's body and dies.

1. CHURL .... selfish
2. HAPLY .... hopefully

"POISON, I SEE, HATH BEEN HIS TIMELESS END."

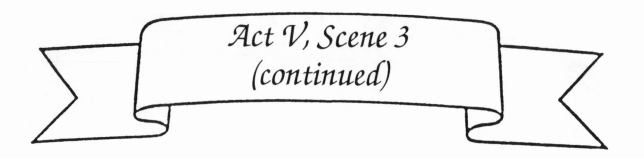

There is a great deal of noise and confusion as the Prince, a guard, Lord Capulet, Lady Capulet and the Friar enter the vault:

GUARD   Sovereign, here lies the County Paris slain;
And Romeo dead; and Juliet, dead before,
Warm and new killed.

Lord Montague enters:

MONTAGUE   Alas, my liege,[1] my wife is dead tonight!
Grief of my son's exile that stopped her breath.
What further woe conspires against mine age?

PRINCE   Look, and thou shalt see.

Montague, already grieving over the death of his wife, is left speechless upon discovering the death of his only child, Romeo. The Friar is left with the dreadful task of explaining everything to the Prince.

1.   LIEGE .... One to whom you owe your allegiance.

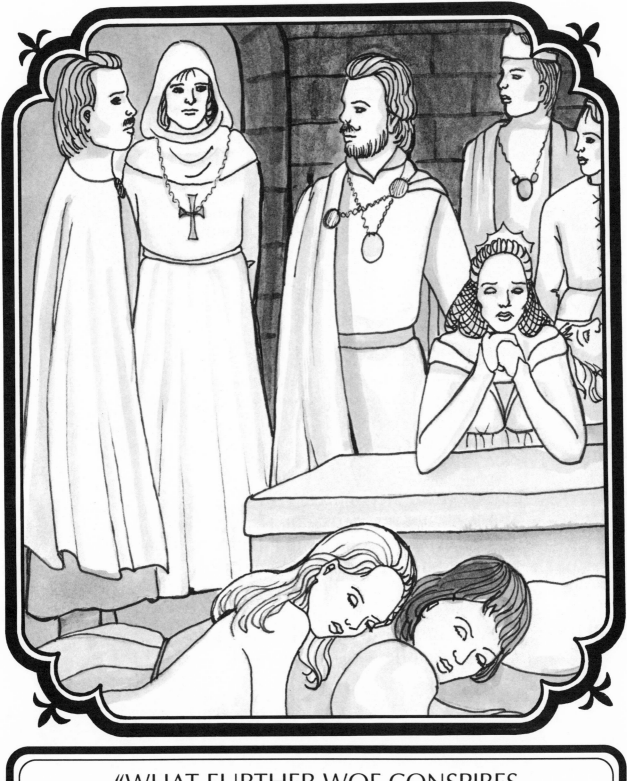

"WHAT FURTHER WOE CONSPIRES
AGAINST MINE AGE?"

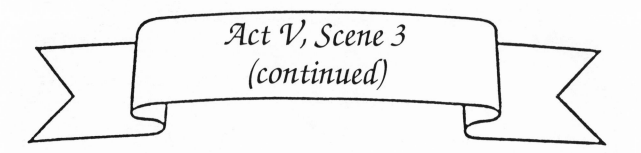

The Prince points out to the Capulets and Montagues how much death and suffering has come from their mutual hatred and their inability to solve their problems without resorting to violence:

PRINCE   Capulet! Montague!
                See what a scourge[1] is laid upon your hate.

Lords Capulet and Montague can barely bear the loss of their only children. The burning hatred that has filled their hearts for so long has now turned into compassion and forgiveness:

CAPULET   O brother Montague, give me thy hand.

MONTAGUE   I can give thee more:
                For I will raise her statue in pure gold,
                That while Verona by that name is known,
                There shall no figure at such rate be set[2]
                As that of true and faithful Juliet.

CAPULET   As rich shall Romeo's by his Lady's lie –
                Poor sacrifices of our enmity!

1. SCOURGE .... punishment

2. SUCH RATE BE SET .... No statue shall be more valuable or costly then the
       one of Juliet.

"O BROTHER MONTAGUE, GIVE ME THY HAND."

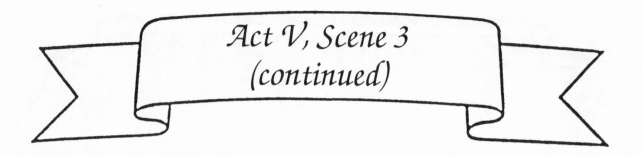

There is silence as Lord Montague and Lord Capulet finally put an end to their bitter and senseless feud. All look upon the dead bodies of Tybalt, Paris, Romeo and Juliet and are reminded of poor Mercutio and the grief-stricken Lady Montague. In spite of the two families finally ending their enmity, there is a terrible and tragic sense of loss as the Prince breaks the silence:

PRINCE A glooming peace this morning with it brings.
The sun for sorrow will not show his head.
Go hence to have more talk of these sad things.
Some shall be pardoned, and some punished,
For never was a story of more woe
Than this of Juliet and her Romeo.

The End

"FOR NEVER WAS A STORY OF MORE WOE THAN THIS OF JULIET AND HER ROMEO."

Discussion Questions

1. The Capulets and Montagues have been feuding for years. The play does not reveal the cause of their feud. Can you think of reasons two families might quarrel?

2. How can those quarrels be resolved without resorting to violence?

3. (Act I, Scene 2) Romeo has grave misgivings about going to the Capulet party, but he let his friends convince him to go. Have you ever done anything you didn't really want to do but let your friends talk you into doing it?

4. What sort of things wouldn't you do, even if your friends wanted you to?

5. (Act I, Scene 3) Juliet's parents want her to marry Paris, a man she has never met. Have you ever been in a situation where a parent or teacher asked you to do something you did not want to do? How did it make you feel?

6. Why do you think you were asked to do that?

7. How do you think Juliet felt about being asked to marry someone she didn't know? Why do you think her parents wanted her to marry Paris? (Remember, in the fourteenth century it was common for parents to determine whom their children would marry.)

8. (Act III, Scene 1) The Prince could have Romeo executed for killing Tybalt, instead Romeo is banished. Romeo's reaction to the news of his banishment (Act III, Scene 3) is that exile is worse than death. Why do you think the thought of exile was so difficult for Romeo?

9. Juliet took a drug (given to her by the Friar) to make it appear she had died. There are a number of adults and children, today, that take drugs. What are some of the consequences of consuming, selling or giving away illegal drugs?

10. Romeo made the foolish choice of killing himself when he thought Juliet was dead. What might have happened if Romeo did not commit suicide?

11. What reasons might compel someone to consider suicide and why is suicide such a poor solution?

12. Which parts of the play made you happy?

13. Which parts of the play made you sad?

14. Which characters did you feel sorry for and why?

15. If you could re-write this play, what would you change?

16. Shakespeare wrote plays to entertain and to teach lessons. What lessons did you learn from this play?

17. If you were to stand in front of your class and describe what you liked most about this play, what would that be?

18. What type of stories or plays are you most interested in?

19. Would you recommend that your best friend read this play?

20. Why?

Cass' SHAKESPEARE FOR CHILDREN
series will soon include:

HAMLET
OTHELLO
MACBETH
CYMBELINE
KING LEAR
THE TEMPEST
AS YOU LIKE IT
HENRY IV, PART I
TAMING OF THE SHREW
MUCH ADO ABOUT NOTHING
A MID SUMMER NIGHT'S DREAM

SIXTY MINUTES OF SHAKESPEARE

Children's theatres, community theatres, secondary and high school teachers, directors and acting students will be happy to learn FIVE STAR PUBLICATIONS will soon be releasing sixty-minute acting editions of many of Shakespeare's plays. The acting editions will contain helpful footnotes and stage directions.

Please check with Five Star Publications for release dates of the continuing SHAKESPEARE FOR CHILDREN series.

Five Star Publications

OTHER FIVE STAR PUBLICATIONS

NANNIES, MAIDS & MORE: The Complete Guide for Hiring Household Help. 1989. Discusses all angles of hiring help on your own, using employment agencies, finding and evaluating day care for children or seniors. Includes many sample forms. Winning natio...
$14.95

OPTIONS: A Directory of ... wide directory listing services specializing in child or sen... of nanny schools and nanny agencies.
$14.95

THE DOMESTIC SCREENIN... ...sehold help. Contains all the forms necessary for screenin... ...l attention.
$24.95

Order any of ... ...ndling.

SHAKESPEARE FOR CHILD... Discussion of Shakespeare'... drama activities. ISBN 0-9...
...re's time and life. 2. ...questions. 5. Creative
$30.00

SHAKESPEARE COLORIN...
$3.95

SIXTY MINUTES OF SHAK... stage directions. ISBN 0-9...
...des helpful footnotes and
$6.95

Please use this ... ...upcoming books.

Name _____
Address _____
City _____ Zip _____
Phone _____

Number of books ordered

		Cost
_____	Shakespeare for	$14.95
_____	Nannies, Maids	14.95
_____	Options: A Dire	14.95
_____	The Domestic S	24.95
_____	PRE PUBLICATI	30.00
_____		3.95
_____		6.95

SUBTOTAL _____

DISCOUNT: (Order three or more books and receive a 10% discount) _____

POSTAGE & HANDLING: ($2 for the first book, $.75 for each additional) _____

TOTAL DUE _____

Mail your order to: **FIVE STAR PUBLICATIONS, Box 3142, Scottsdale, AZ 85271-3142** or charge your order and call toll-free **1-800-545-STAR, ext. 14.** Please have your charge card handy. Mastercard, Visa, & American Express welcome.